W9-CON-446

A POLK STREET SPECIAL

Next Stop, New York City!

Patricia Reilly Giff

Illustrated by Blanche Sims

A Yearling Book

Published by
Bantam Doubleday Dell Books for Young Readers
a division of
Bantam Doubleday Dell Publishing Group, Inc.
1540 Broadway
New York, New York 10036

ISBN: 0-440-41362-1
Printed in the United States of America
June 1997
10 9 8 7 6 5 4 3 2 1
CWO

For all my Jims—
with love

Chapter 1

It was Pizzazz Week at the Polk Street School.

Emily Arrow was wearing new plaid socks today, purple ones.

She pulled out her red, white, and blue notebook. She slapped an American flag sticker on top. *June 14th*, said the sticker. *Flag Day*.

"I'm full of pizzazz," Matthew said from across the aisle.

"I'm full of Planters peanuts." Beast opened his mouth wide.

"Yucks," said Matthew.

"Double yucks." Emily wiggled her toes in her purple socks. Something with pizzazz was going to happen today. A Ms. Rooney surprise.

Ms. Rooney was going to tell them about it any minute.

Emily squinted up at the ceiling. It was probably something to do with flags. The class had been studying them for ages.

Red, white, and blue for the United States of America. A red leaf for Canada. A blue star for Israel.

Emily looked around. Jill Simon was standing at the side of the room. One of her four braids was coming out. One of her bows was missing.

Poor Jill had as much pizzazz as Harry, the class fish.

It looked as if Jill was ready to cry. Emily wondered why.

She didn't have much time to wonder. Ms. Rooney was clapping her hands.

Emily sat up straight. The surprise was coming.

Ms. Rooney pointed to her feet. "These are my traveling shoes."

Emily caught her breath. They were going to travel somewhere. Ms. Rooney loved class trips. What pizzazz!

"I'd like to travel right out of here," said Beast.

"Where would you go?" Ms. Rooney was smiling. She didn't seem to mind that Beast was interrupting.

"I'd travel to . . . ," Beast began, and stopped. "Uhm—"

"Florida," Dawn Bosco cut in. "That's where my grandmother lives. That's where I got these." She pointed to her seashell earrings. "Gorgeous, right?"

Emily made a fish face. Dawn Bosco thought she had more pizzazz than a princess.

Ms. Rooney picked up a piece of pink chalk. "Anyone want to tell us about their travels?"

Derrick Grace told about visiting the Red River Valley. Alex Walker told about San Francisco's Golden Gate Bridge.

"I'm heading straight for the planet Pluto," Matthew said.

"Ssh-oom," Beast yelled.

Emily tried to look as if she were thinking of a place with pizzazz. Too bad. The best she could think of was the Ice Cream Igloo.

Now Ms. Rooney was drawing pink shoes with pointy toes. And underneath:

THINK ABOUT YOUR TRAVELING SHOES.
WRITE ABOUT A PLACE YOU'VE BEEN
WITH YOUR FAMILY.
MAKE US FEEL AS IF WE HAVE
TRAVELING SHOES.

Was that going to be their homework?

Emily sighed. Some pizzazz that was.

She looked toward the side of the room. Jill Simon was still there. She was trying to get Dawn Bosco's attention. "Psst," she said.

In two seconds Dawn was standing next to Jill. She had a pencil in her hand.

Ms. Rooney probably thought she was sharpening it.

Emily narrowed her eyes. Dawn's pencil was sharp as a tack.

"Ms. Rooney," Dawn called. "Look at this."

Emily stood up. Beast and Matthew jumped over their seats to get to the side of the room.

Even Ms. Rooney was coming around from in front.

Suddenly Emily had a worried feeling. It was hard to swallow.

She guessed what they were looking at.

Everyone was leaning over the "This Is Life" table.

"Blech," said Beast.

"Ruined," said Dawn Bosco.

Emily was the last one to the table. She stood on tiptoes to see over Beast's head.

All their "This Is Life" plants were dead.

"Poor dried-up scrunchy things," said Jill.

Emily closed her eyes.

Jim, the custodian, was painting the hall for Pizzazz Week.

Herman, his helper, was putting in new lights.

And Emily's class was growing plants for the hall.

Ms. Rooney frowned. "Who is the plant monitor?"

Emily began to raise her hand.

"Sherri Dent has been absent all week," said Jill. "Maybe . . ."

Emily put her hand down.

"What a shame." Ms. Rooney shook her head.

Emily went back to her seat. Her heart was pounding.

She should have told them who the *real* plant monitor was.

Emily had forgotten to water the plants for the whole week.

This was the worst day she could remember.

But then came Ms. Rooney's surprise. "In a few days, we're hopping on a bus," she said. "We're heading straight for New York City."

"We'll see all the flags," said Beast.

It might be wonderful, Emily thought. If only she could do tonight's homework. And what could she do about Sherri Dent?

Chapter 2

Emily went into the kitchen. "I have to think," she told her mother.

"About New York City?" her mother asked.

"No." Emily shook her head. "Hey, how did you know we were going?"

Her mother laughed. "Mothers know everything."

Baby Katie was in her high chair. She was laughing too. Emily leaned over for a kiss.

Emily cooed back. "You've got pizzazz, Katie."

Katie began to bang her keys on the high chair.

"I can't think down here," Emily told her mother.

"I wonder why," said her mother.

Emily went up to her bedroom. She closed the door.

"Too loud," her little sister Stacy said from under her bed. "I'm trying to think."

"Whoever heard of thinking under a bed?" Emily asked.

Stacy poked her head out. She had a dust ball in her hair. "It's dark under here, and quiet."

Emily sat on her bed. Maybe Sherri Dent would be back in school tomorrow.

She'd stick her pointy nose in the air. "I wasn't the plant monitor," she'd say. "It was Emily Arrow."

Emily bit at her lip. She was going to be in the worst trouble.

She slid under her own bed. Stacy was right. It was dark under there, and quiet.

There was a secret too: an old purse with the quarters she was saving.

Emily thought about New York City. Maybe they'd see an Irish flag. That was her favorite. Next to the American flag, of course.

She closed her eyes. Homework. Where had she ever gone?

They had stayed at her aunt Caroline's on winter break last year. That was in a place called the Bronx, wherever that was.

Aunt Caroline had a huge apartment. It was made out of an old movie house.

Instead of popcorn, it smelled like pizza.

It smelled of fish water too. Aunt Caroline had fish swimming around in tanks.

Aunt Caroline's apartment didn't count. It didn't have pizzazz like Florida or the Red

River Valley. It certainly wasn't like the planet Pluto.

"Stacy," Emily asked, "can you think of a place we've gone? A place far from home? Like Aunt Caroline's, but—"

"Don't talk to me about Aunt Caroline's house," Stacy said. "It smells of pizza . . . and something else too."

"Fish water," Emily said. "Where else?"

"How about when we went to Mrs. Larkin's?"

Stacy was no help. Mrs. Larkin lived two houses away.

Emily thought of the places she had been. Adventure Land. Snow Park. And class trips.

She couldn't write about those places. Everyone knew about them.

Downstairs the door opened. Emily could hear Stacy scramble out from under the bed.

"Daddy's home," Stacy said.

Emily slid out too. She raced down the

stairs. She'd ask her father about a place they'd gone. He always remembered everything.

Her father was in the kitchen. He was still wearing his police uniform. He was swinging Katie around.

Katie was smiling at her father. Her arms were tight around his neck.

"I need . . . ," Emily began.

Now Stacy was wrapping herself around his legs. They were all laughing.

"Hey, guys . . . ," Emily began.

No one heard her. The kitchen was filled with noise.

She tried one more time. "Hey . . . ," she began. Her father patted her head. He kept twirling around.

Then it was dinnertime.

"Listen," Emily asked everyone at the table, "can you tell me a place we've been?"

"That again?" Stacy asked.

Her father looked up at the ceiling. "Easy. Aunt Caroline's."

Emily piled up a mountain of peas. She made a volcano with her fork.

Stacy was telling a story about a horse she had seen. "Two tails," she said. "One in front and one in back."

"I saw one with three ears," said her father.

Emily tried to think of something funny to say.

She couldn't think of one thing. She ate a few peas instead.

By the time she remembered to say that Aunt Caroline's was no good at all, it was too late.

Now her mother blasted water into the sink. She was singing a song about Barney Google.

Her father was dancing with Katie.

Stacy was eating the jelly out of the cookies.

Emily sat watching, smiling. Her whole family had pizzazz. Then she touched her plain no-earrings ears.

Even with her purple socks, she didn't have pizzazz. She might be like Jill Simon and Harry the fish.

Maybe she didn't have one bit of pizzazz at all.

Chapter 3

Emily hurried across the schoolyard. She looked up at the flag. Some people called it Old Glory.

What a neat name. It made her happy to think of it.

Then she remembered. Suppose Sherri Dent was back?

She started down the hall. Walk slow as a snail, she told herself.

She looked through the window in the door. She could see words on the chalkboard: DON'T FORGET . . .

She couldn't see what she shouldn't forget. Matthew was in the way. He was jumping up and down like a frog. The back of his shirt was erasing everything.

What she did see was Sherri Dent's empty desk.

Whew. She went inside. She passed Drake and Harry's fish tank. Drake was mean and tough. Poor Harry was gray with stripes.

Emily looked down at her shirt. It was gray with stripes too.

Emily slid into her seat next to Dawn Bosco.

Dawn put her lunch bag on top of her notebook. "No looking," she told Emily.

Emily popped her lips. "Who wants to look?"

Up in front, Ms. Rooney closed her eyes.

"Do I hear good friends fighting? I'm speech-less."

Emily put her hands up to her mouth. She had forgotten. Last week had been Good Friends Week.

Emily sighed. She wasn't a good friend to Sherri Dent. She should raise her hand right this minute and say, "I was the plant moni-tor."

She shivered thinking about it.

Now Ms. Rooney was drawing another pair of shoes. White sneakers with red laces.

Everyone was getting out travel stories. They were raising their hands.

Emily got hers out too. She had written it this morning . . . so fast there was a dot of Lucky Charms cereal on one edge.

Beast slapped his forehead. "I forgot mine."

Ms. Rooney shook her head. "I'm glad it's not Really Responsible Week."

"Me too," said Beast.

Dawn Bosco went to the front. "Florida," she said. *"F-L-O-R-I-D-A.* In case you want to spell it."

Emily didn't want to spell *Florida.* Instead she looked up at the chalkboard: DON'T FORGET . . .

She squished her eyes together. She could just see the next words: NEXT SUNDAY IS . . .

Dawn was telling things about Florida.

"Alligators, really?" Beast was saying. "Wow."

"And Sea World," said Dawn.

Wait till the class heard about her own travel, Emily thought. Yucks and double yucks.

"Yes," said Ms. Rooney at last. "Dawn is our expert on Florida."

Next came Timothy Barbiero. Timothy was the expert on New Jersey.

After a while, Emily had all the experts mixed up.

Then it was her turn.

She opened her notebook. She went to the front.

She took a breath just the way Stacy told her. She smiled too.

"Everyone will think Aunt Caroline's isn't that bad," Stacy had said at breakfast.

"Really?" Emily had said, thinking it over. "Maybe you're right."

She began to read:

> *My aunt Caroline lives in a place called the Bronx.*

She looked at Dawn Bosco. "*B-R-A-N-K-S*, in case you want to spell it."

She could see Ms. Rooney shaking her head, no.

Emily shook her head a little too. How

could anyone know how to spell a word like that?

Emily began to read again:

> *Aunt Caroline's apartment is big.*
> *She has a million fish.*
> *A pizza place is downstairs.*

"Lovely," said Ms. Rooney. "Now, does anyone know where the Bronx is?"

Emily opened her mouth. She closed it again. She made believe she was pulling up her socks. Then she stopped. She didn't want everyone to see. They were plain white. White with a couple of grass stains.

"Planet Pluto?" asked Matthew.

"The Big Apple," said Ms. Rooney. "That's what people call New York City."

Emily blinked. She couldn't believe it. Aunt Caroline lived in New York City.

Even Dawn Bosco looked surprised.

"Emily Arrow is our New York City expert," said Ms. Rooney.

Beast slid down on the floor. "I'm speechless," he said.

What next? thought Emily. She didn't know one thing about New York City . . . except pizza, and fish water, and Aunt Caroline's apartment.

Ms. Rooney was still talking. "We'll stay overnight. . . ."

Dawn was talking too. "I'm going to bring my number one pajamas."

"Poor Sherri," said Linda. "I wonder if she'll be back."

Dawn nodded. "I hope so . . . even if she is a plant killer."

Emily bent over to pull up her socks again.

"New York has flags all over the place," said Ms. Rooney. "And . . ."

"New York has everything all over the place," said Timothy Barbiero.

"And the P.T.O. is giving us the money."
Ms. Rooney tapped the board with her chalk.
"We'll march in a parade. Don't forget that
Sunday is June fourteenth. . . ."

Emily took a breath. She could just see the
words: FLAG DAY.

"The flag's birthday," said Emily.

Ms. Rooney nodded.

"I'm speechless," said Beast.

Chapter 4

Someone was calling. Emily didn't stop. She raced down Stone Street and across Linden. She took a breath at the library door.

Inside, she headed for Miss Bailey's desk. "I need . . . New York City, please."

"You're in a hurry," said the librarian.

Emily nodded. Of course she was in a hurry. She had one day to become a New York City expert.

"Tons of things to see," said Miss Bailey.

Emily's heart sank. How could she be an expert about all those things?

Miss Bailey pointed. "Go to the third stack."

Emily walked past the tables. In back of her Miss Bailey was saying something. Something about the fourth grade doing reports on New York City.

"I hope something is left," Emily called.

Emily crossed her fingers. She could see a fat red apple pasted to the top of one of the shelves.

Yes. She took a breath.

No. She took another breath. The shelf was empty. The books on New York City were gone.

All except for one baby thing on the floor. Even a two-year-old could read it: *The Big Apple for Little Kids.*

Emily picked it up. It was a mess. Pages smushed. Old black-and-white pictures.

"Didn't you hear me?" a voice called.

Emily looked over her shoulder. It was Dawn.

Emily grabbed a fat book from the next shelf. *Plants of the World.* She grabbed another from underneath: *Betsy—Girl of the 1700s.*

She stuck the baby New York City book in between. "Hi, Dawn," she said.

Dawn slid to a stop. "You're looking at plant stuff?"

"Yes," Emily said. *Plants of the World* looked like the boringest book she had ever seen. Ant-sized letters, elephant-sized words. It had no pictures at all.

"I'm an expert on fat books," Dawn said.

Emily stuck her nose in the air. "Me too." Too bad she was an expert on nothing, she thought.

"I thought you were an expert on New York City." Dawn leaned a little closer. "I think it's terrible about our 'This Is Life' plant table."

Emily nodded.

"Poor squished-up plants," Dawn said. "All dumped in the garbage."

Emily kept nodding.

"Died of thirst," Dawn said.

"Yes," said Emily.

"Sherri should have come back to take care of them."

"Maybe Sherri is too sick . . ."

"Probably just a cold," Dawn said.

"Probably double ear infections," said Emily.

"Really Responsible Week starts next week," said Dawn. "Sherri is going to be out of luck." She began to flip through a book.

Emily flipped too. It was all her fault. Poor Sherri. Poor sick Sherri, she thought.

At last Dawn wandered away.

Emily counted to five. She peered around the corner. Dawn was at a table reading a gigantic book.

Emily didn't waste any time. She rushed back to the librarian's desk. She took quick looks over her shoulder. Dawn was reading a mile a minute.

At last Miss Bailey checked out the three books. "I love plants," she said. "Don't you?"

"I guess so," Emily said.

Miss Bailey tapped the other book, the Betsy book. "I loved this one too. Can you imagine? There were ten children in Betsy Griscom's family. They couldn't all fit at the dinner table at once."

Emily walked home opening a pack of Life Savers she had found in her pocket. She thought about being in a family with ten children.

She sat on the back steps. By the time she had eaten the last two Life Savers, she had finished the New York book too.

Stacy banged outside. "Want to read to me?"

Emily turned the book over, ready to begin again.

"Isn't that a baby thing?" Stacy asked.

"It's about New York City," Emily said. "It's a bunch of islands. Manhattan is one. Staten Island is another. Queens and Brooklyn are on Long Island. And there's one piece stuck on the mainland. That's called the Bronx."

"That's called boring," Stacy said.

Emily thought it was boring too. "New York is called the city that never sleeps."

"You're putting me to sleep." Stacy began to laugh at her own joke.

"Well . . . ," Emily said. "It has good parts. It's mostly about Manhattan. That's one of the islands."

Inside, Emily could hear the phone ringing.

Stacy hopped up the back step.

" 'New York has six thousand miles of

streets, seven of the world's tallest buildings, more than seven hundred miles of subways . . . ,' " Emily read before Stacy disappeared into the house.

The screen banged shut. Emily heard Stacy pick up the phone.

" 'Twenty million miles of telephone wires . . . ,' " Emily read anyway.

Stacy poked her head out. "It's for you, Emily," she said. "It's Sherri Dent."

Chapter 5

Emily picked up the phone. She could hardly talk.

"Hello," Sherri was yelling. "Hello?"

"It's me," said Emily after a minute. "Did you call about the . . ." She couldn't even finish.

"I called about the trip," said Sherri. "I called because you were supposed to bring me my homework."

"No," Emily began. And then she remembered. "I'm sorry," she said. "Really . . ."

"It's a good thing Jill Simon called," Sherri said. "She told me the news. . . ."

"About the plants?" Emily said.

"Plants?" Sherri asked.

"The 'This Is Life' table," Emily said, her eyes closed.

"I'll bet those babies are growing like crazy," said Sherri.

"Well . . ."

"Well, I called to ask you to be my partner."

Emily smiled. "I'm glad you picked me," she said.

"You were the only one left," said Sherri.

Emily didn't hear the rest. She said good-bye after a moment.

The only one left.

"I knew it," she told baby Katie in

her swing. "I don't have one bit of pizzazz."

Her mother was in the kitchen. She held up a pair of pajamas. The tops didn't match the bottoms. "Great for your New York City trip," her mother said. "Not too warm, not too cool."

"Not any pizzazz." Emily went upstairs. She could hear her mother laughing.

All her clothes were out on the bed. They were ready for her suitcase.

Emily put her Betsy book and the fat plant book on top.

Then she went over to the dresser. Three pictures were lined up on top. Katie was showing her one tooth. Stacy was curling her hair against her fingers.

They both looked wonderful.

Emily's was the third picture. Straight-as-a-stick brown hair, brown eyes, no smile.

Emily leaned closer. "No-pizzazz pajamas for a no-pizzazz girl," she said.

The picture Emily looked back. "And," Emily began, "you're not a good friend to Sherri."

Stacy popped her head out from under the bed. "When you talk to yourself, you should talk more quietly."

Emily jumped.

"Why don't you wear your number one pajamas from last winter?" Stacy asked.

"Do you think I want to boil to death?" Emily asked.

"Boiled like a lobster," Stacy said, chuckling. She went under the bed again.

Emily opened her dresser drawers. Not in the first one. Not in the second.

They were in the third drawer, fuzzy pajamas with a big red heart.

Emily threw them on top of the pile of clothes.

Then she went over to the mirror.

She smiled as hard as she could. She looked like a . . .

"Shark face," Stacy said, her face peeking out from the bedspread.

Emily smiled a smaller smile.

It wasn't any better.

She still looked like a no-pizzazz, no-good-friend girl.

Chapter 6

It was Friday. Emily bumped her suitcase down the stairs.

Her mother was in the kitchen. "A special breakfast," she said.

"Bagels and cream cheese," said Emily.

"New Yorkers love bagels," her mother said. "Maybe you'll bring a couple home for us."

"Bring a pile," Stacy said. She was cutting out a paper chair for her doll Glennie.

"In my book Betsy made doll furniture too," Emily told her.

Emily ate her breakfast and kissed everyone goodbye.

Her mother gave her a hug. "You're going to get a neat surprise in New York City."

Emily opened her mouth. "What . . ." But her father was hustling her out the door and into the car.

In almost no time, she was standing in front of school. A bus was waiting at the gate. Kids were running all over the place.

Beast was playing Got You Last with Matthew.

Derrick was snapping pictures of the flag that was flying in front of the school.

Emily looked up at the flag too. It was waving in the wind.

Then she spotted Dawn. Dawn was wearing a baseball hat with a pink rose.

Emily made a fish face. Too bad she hadn't thought of a baseball hat.

Now she could see Alex Walker's father talking with Noni, Dawn's grandmother. They were going on the trip too.

Emily could see Sherri Dent coming toward her. Her mouth felt dry.

But there was no time for anyone to say anything. No time for anyone to say, *"You killed the plants, Sherri."*

The bus driver was calling. It was time to board.

Emily found a seat with Sherri. Sherri looked pale. All except for her pointy nose.

It was red as Rudolph's.

A moment later, Linda Lorca and Dawn slid into seats in front of them. They leaned over the seats and began to talk.

"If I were sick," Dawn said, "I'd still come in to water—"

"Fasten your seat belts," the bus driver said.

"It's almost Really Responsible Week," said Linda.

Sherri looked surprised. "What?"

But the driver was swinging the bus around. Dawn and Linda had to buckle up.

Emily crossed her fingers. Maybe they'd forget about Sherri and the plants.

Across the aisle, Noni smiled at Emily. "I came to this country from Italy," she said. "I took a ship to New York. I wanted to be an American citizen."

Dawn stood up. "I'm just going to stand in the aisle," she said. "I can see a little better."

Noni frowned. "Being a good citizen means doing what you're supposed to. It's being responsible."

Dawn sank back into her seat again. Emily could see the pink flower on her hat bobbing up and down.

Emily pulled out her Betsy book. The bus was bumping along. It was hard to read.

Emily looked at the pictures instead.

They weren't real pictures. They were drawings: Betsy sewing. Betsy grown up and meeting her husband, John Ross.

Sherri opened her eyes. She saw Emily's plant book. "Mind if I look?" she asked. "I love plants."

"Hmpfh," Dawn Bosco said in front of them.

Sherri flipped through the pages. "My grandmother taught me about plants," she said. "Some need a lot of light. Some need a lot of water."

The bus driver tapped the horn. "The Fifty-ninth Street Bridge is coming up," he yelled. "You'll see New York City in two minutes."

What Emily saw was a pile of cars.

"Maybe our New York City expert can tell us about the buildings," Ms. Rooney said.

Emily looked around for the New York City expert.

Then she gulped. Ms. Rooney was talking to her.

Emily dived for her baby book. She looked up. She could see buildings from the side of the bridge. Huge blocks of buildings. Beautiful gray and white ones with needle-thin tops.

Emily took a peek at the book. "We're going to cross a bridge. We'll go over the East River."

Next to the bridge, a thin wire was stretched high in the air. A funny-looking car hung from the wire.

People were looking out the car windows.

"Cool," said Beast. "They're going to zip across the river."

Emily's hands felt damp. She'd hate to be up so high. "It's the Roosevelt Island Tram," she said.

Ms. Rooney turned around. "I'm speechless, Emily. You really are a New York City expert."

"I'd rather live in Florida," Dawn said.

The bus had crossed the bridge now. It went along a skinny street. The street was filled with people.

It was filled with cars and taxis too.

It took the bus a half hour to move two inches.

Emily kept watching out the window. A man was selling hot dogs. A boy on Rollerblades sailed past.

Then Emily saw a building that was in her book. "It's Madison Square Garden," she said. "Lots of things happen there . . . prizefights, and ice shows . . . and there's a railroad station underneath . . ."

Mr. Walker was nodding, smiling. "Wait. I want to show Alex. I want to show all of you." He asked the bus driver, "Can you stop?"

A minute later they were inside. They went down an escalator into the station. Hundreds of people were hurrying for trains. They looked like a line of busy ants. They had come from places all over the country.

"I lived on a farm when I was little," Mr. Walker said. "When I grew up, I wanted to come to New York City. I took the train here to . . ."

"Pennsylvania Station," Emily said.

"Yes," said Mr. Walker. "I never saw so many people. First I wanted to go home." He put his hand on Alex's head. "And then I saw my cousins . . . ten of them . . . waiting for me. New York was my new home."

It made Emily think of Betsy Ross with all her brothers and sisters.

She didn't have much time to think.

Ms. Rooney was telling everyone they had to get back on the bus.

Dawn had raced across the station to look

at a bookstore window. Noni snapped her fingers. "Responsibility," she called.

Emily went up the escalator. She didn't want to think about responsibility. She didn't want to think about being a good friend. She felt sad about Sherri.

Sometime on this trip Sherri would find out about the plants.

The class marched back to the bus.

Emily knew what she had to do.

She had to tell Sherri about the plant business.

But how?

And suppose Sherri told everyone else?

Chapter 7

The bus was moving again. Emily opened her Betsy book.

Betsy was working in a shop now, with her husband, John Ross. It was a shop that made pillows and chair cushions.

"Can you guess where we are?" Ms. Rooney asked a few minutes later.

Everyone was shaking their head, no.

Even Noah Greene and Timothy Barbiero, the smartest kids in the class.

Emily looked out the window. On one side of the street were hotel buildings. She could see the American flag and a white one with a big red sun.

"That's the Japanese flag," said Ms. Rooney.

The bus slowed down. "Take a look," said the bus driver.

On the other side of the street was a park. A huge park. Kids sped by on bikes. Mothers pushed baby strollers.

"It's Central Park," Emily said. "Right in the middle of the city."

"Give me Florida," said Dawn Bosco.

"Give me the planet Pluto," said Matthew.

"Give me a punch in the nose," said Beast.

The bus stopped on the next street. Emily saw something on the front of a building.

THE AMERICAN MUSEUM . . .

Emily opened her mouth again. "The

American Museum of Natural History," she said.

"Yes," said Ms. Rooney.

"Anyone would know that," Dawn said. "It's written in the stone."

"Good friends," Ms. Rooney reminded them.

"And good friends to plants too." Linda stared at Sherri.

"We get off here," Ms. Rooney said. "Stay with your partner."

Inside, Emily began to search through her book. There were two pictures on the museum page.

She looked at the first one. "I hope we're going to see the Indian canoe," she said, "and the totem pole."

Ms. Rooney looked back. "Wonderful, Emily," she said. "I'm glad you're getting a surprise tonight."

"Surprise?" Emily asked. Someone else

had said something like that. And then she remembered. Her mother. "What?"

Ms. Rooney smiled. "Wait and see."

The flower on Dawn's hat was shaking back and forth. "Surprise?" she asked.

"Yes," said Ms. Rooney. "But maybe Emily will like it best."

"Hmff," said Dawn.

"I'm speechless," said Beast.

Emily followed Sherri down the hall. She wished she were Betsy Ross. She'd be sewing furniture in her shop. She wouldn't be worried about Sherri.

She took another peek at the book. All she had time to see was a picture of Betsy with George Washington.

Meeting the first American president, thought Emily. Now that had pizzazz. And he was asking her to make a flag for the country.

The class walked through a room with a

bunch of huge bones stuck together. A monster towered over them.

"It's a *Tyrannosaurus rex*," said Beast. "He's out to get you."

"It's Superdino," said Matthew. "He'll probably chew your head off."

And a little farther along, Linda was saying, "Hey look, bison."

Emily looked into a window. She could see a bunch of fat animals.

"They look like cows," Jill Simon said. "Except their hair is curly."

"And look at the plants," said Sherri. "Grasses and cactuses."

Emily nodded a little.

"I loved it when I was plant monitor last month," Sherri said. "I think plants are my favorite things."

"Think again," said Dawn.

"Time for lunch," Noni was saying.

Emily headed for the Food Express. Sherri marched along beside her.

In back, Jill was saying, "We'll all sit together."

That was the last thing Emily wanted to do.

Instead, she and Sherri sat in seats next to Derrick.

Maybe he'd take their pictures.

Chapter 8

Emily tried not to yawn. She walked on the sides of her feet.

It seemed as if they had walked forever today. They'd seen Fifth Avenue with beautiful stores.

They had stood in line to whoosh to the top of the Empire State Building. They had seen German and Mexican and British flags flying from the windows.

The British one was red, white, and blue like the American.

"My favorite part is coming next," said Noni, Dawn's grandmother.

The bus stopped at another park.

"Battery Park," said Emily.

"And a ferry ride," said Ms. Rooney. "We'll get to see the Statue of Liberty up close."

It was a huge boat, Emily thought. It had room for cars, and people walking around, and . . .

Mr. Walker was handing out hats, green Statue of Liberty hats.

"Remember," said Noni, "I came to the United States on a ship from Italy. It took a long time, and I was seasick. I was homesick too."

Emily nodded.

"And then . . ." Noni pointed.

"The Statue of Liberty," Emily said.

"Yes," Noni said. "It was the first thing I saw in this country."

Everyone was staring at the statue.

Emily stared the hardest. She wanted to tell Stacy all about it. She wanted to tell her it was just like the pictures . . . a giant lady holding a torch.

"After a few years, I could speak English well," Noni said. "I went to the courthouse. I promised I would be a good citizen."

After the ferry ride, the class sat down for a minute to rest.

Emily kept thinking about being a good citizen. It was time to tell Sherri. "Listen, Sherri," she said. "I did something terrible."

Sherri opened her purse. She pulled out a cough drop. "Here, you'll feel better."

Emily reached for one.

"Don't worry," Sherri was saying. "Everyone does something terrible sometimes."

"But I did something terrible to you," Emily whispered.

Sherri pulled back the cough drop box. "What?"

"I was the plant monitor this week," Emily began.

"I hope you watered them a lot," Sherri said. "Violets need tons of water."

The class was walking again.

Linda marched past. "Plant killer."

"Very sad," said Dawn. She marched past them too.

Sherri's mouth was open. "You killed our plants for 'This Is Life'?"

Emily opened her mouth. "I—"

"The ones we were growing for Pizzazz Week at the Polk Street School?"

"Yes," Emily said. She watched the class march into a bakery. A green, white, and red flag was flying over the front.

"It's the Italian flag," said Ms. Rooney.

"Dawn is right," said Sherri. "That's very sad. Poor plants. Poor Polk Street School."

"Yes," said Emily.

Ms. Rooney was counting noses. "Seven . . . eight . . ."

They stood at the counter. Behind a window were pastries and cookies.

"I'm going to have a hundred," said Beast.

"A thousand," said Matthew.

"I have to tell you something else," Emily told Sherri.

Sherri wasn't paying attention. "I can't make up my mind," she said. "Everything looks wonderful."

Emily leaned toward Sherri.

She didn't lean too close. She didn't want to catch double ear infections.

"Everyone thinks you were the plant monitor," Emily whispered. "I didn't tell them it was me."

Sherri stood there for a moment. She stared

at Emily. Then she stuck her pointy nose in the air.

"You were right," she said. "That was terrible."

She stepped around Emily. "Wait up," she told Dawn and Linda. "I'm going to sit with you guys."

"Could I wait outside?" Emily asked Ms. Rooney. "Right in front?"

Ms. Rooney nodded. "Don't move a muscle away from the door," she said.

Emily nodded. She stood in the doorway. She didn't move a muscle until everyone came back outside.

Chapter 9

They were back on the bus again. Sherri was sitting in the seat next to Emily. She was sitting as far away as she could.

Emily looked down at her Betsy book. Betsy was sewing stars. "Five points are better than six," she was telling George Washington. "I'll sew white stars on a blue background. One star for each of the thirteen states."

Only thirteen states, Emily thought. Ms. Rooney had told them there were fifty states now.

She wished she could show the picture of Betsy Ross to Sherri.

She wished she could talk to Sherri.

Emily swallowed. She could see Ms. Rooney smiling. "It's almost time for the surprise," she said.

The bus inched along. Outside, Emily could see the East River again.

A tugboat was pushing a barge. The barge was filled with garbage.

"Yuck," said Jill Simon.

"There are so many people," Ms. Rooney was saying. "That means tons of garbage. The barge is taking it away."

Ms. Rooney looked at Emily. "Can you guess where we're heading?"

Emily sighed. She wished they were going home. She wanted to crawl under her bed.

She wanted to be in the dark and quiet with the dust balls.

Ms. Rooney was still looking at Emily. "We're going to the Bronx," she said.

Emily nodded. She closed her eyes. She didn't open them again until she felt the bus stop.

In front of them was a restaurant. A green sign blinked on and off. PEPPERONI PIZZA. BEST IN THE BRONX.

Emily sat up straight. The sign reminded her of something. She couldn't think what it was.

Then she saw the apartment house next door. "That's . . . ," she began.

Someone was hurrying out the front door.

"Here comes the surprise," said Ms. Rooney.

"I'm getting my camera ready," said Derrick.

Ms. Rooney smiled. "We're staying here tonight."

"It's my aunt Caroline." Emily couldn't believe it.

"Her aunt lives in a movie house?" Dawn said. "That Emily has all the luck."

Aunt Caroline stuck her head in the door. "I have sleeping bags on the old stage," she said. "I have pizza. And I have a kiss for my favorite niece, Emily Arrow."

"Great surprise," said Beast.

Everyone was piling out of the bus. Emily stood up. She went to the front of the bus to give Aunt Caroline a hug.

Ms. Rooney was right. It was a wonderful surprise.

Even if the whole class never spoke to her again, she had Aunt Caroline.

"I'm glad to be here," Emily told her.

Everyone else was happy to be there too.

Kids were running around, jumping over sleeping bags. They were eating tons of pizza and salad.

Everything smelled like pizza, Emily thought, with a little fish water mixed in.

She looked around. Ms. Rooney had her feet up. Her polka-dot dress had a spot of tomato sauce. Her hair wasn't puffy anymore.

Noni sat in an armchair with her eyes closed. Mr. Walker looked half-asleep too.

The rest of the kids were watching the fish.

"Guppies," said Aunt Caroline. "I have thousands."

Emily sighed. There was still something else she had to say to Sherri.

She looked around. Sherri was standing at a fish tank in the hall.

"I forgot," Emily said. "I wanted to say I'm sorry."

Sherri didn't look friendly. She looked sad. She looked as if she was going to cry. "Last week was Good Friends Week," she said.

Emily put her head down.

"Wait," said Sherri. "There's something I have to tell you too."

Emily didn't wait. She ran to find her number one pajamas. She knew she was going to cry.

Chapter 10

It was morning again. Aunt Caroline gave
flags to everyone in the class. "Wave these
at the parade," she said.

Now Mr. Walker stood in the middle of the
street. He held his hand up to the traffic. Ms.
Rooney's class crossed from one side to the
other.

They were heading for the Flag Day
Parade. Even from three blocks away, Emily
could hear the sound of drums.

"Mr. Mancina will want to hear about the parade," said Ms. Rooney. "We'll have to remember everything."

Emily could hear a bugle now. The whole class was hurrying down the street.

Sherri Dent was in back of her. Emily turned. Sherri's pointy nose was turned up, but there were tears in her eyes.

"I did something terrible," Sherri said.

Emily reached into her pocket. She found a Life Saver. "Here," she said. "Take one." She had to shout over the noise of the drums.

She heard bits and pieces of what Sherri said. "You forgot about my homework and I wanted to pay you back. I said you were the last one . . ."

Emily shouted back. "For a partner?"

"That everyone was taken . . . that no one had asked you. It was a fib. . . ."

Emily took a breath. A fib. She couldn't be-

lieve it. "I have no pizzazz anyway," she said.

"What?" Sherri asked.

Emily yelled over the drums. "I have no pizzazz."

Beast was right behind her. "You're shouting in my ear," he said, but he was laughing. "You have lots of pizzazz. You're a New York expert . . ."

Emily was shaking her head. "I killed the 'This Is Life' plants."

"Don't worry," Sherri said. "I'm a plant expert. What we need are desert plants. They don't need much water. We can forget about them. It won't matter."

"I'm a desert animal," said Beast. "A lizard."

"You look like a cactus," said Matthew.

Emily took a breath. After the parade they were going to the Bronx's New York Botanical Garden.

She thought of something. She could use her quarters for some desert plants.

On the way home she'd tell the class all about Betsy Ross and the first flag.

And she wanted to hear more about Noni's story.

The parade was right in front of them. Emily stood on tiptoes to watch. It was wonderful to be here in the Big Apple.

The Polk Street
Guide to
New York City

Ms. Rooney says:

"Get on your traveling shoes. Tell us about New York City . . ."

The Polk Street Kids' Favorite Places to See and Things to Do in New York City
(listed in alphabetical order)

Map of the Five Boroughs *84*

Map of Lower Manhattan *92*

Map of Mid- and Upper Manhattan *102*

American Craft Museum 109

American Museum of Natural History 110

Baseball 89

Battery Park City 93

Bronx Zoo (International Wildlife
Conservation Park) 118

Brooklyn Children's Museum 117

Central Park 105

Children's Museum of Manhattan 113

Circle Line Cruise 90

The Cloisters 116

Ellis Island Immigration Museum 95

Empire State Building 100

Federal Hall National Memorial
and Museum 96

Forbes Magazine Galleries 99
Grand Central Terminal 101
Solomon R. Guggenheim Museum 112
Harlem 115
Intrepid Sea-Air-Space Museum 91
Jewish Museum 118
Lincoln Center for the Performing Arts 111
Lower East Side Tenement Museum 99
Metropolitan Museum of Art 112
El Museo del Barrio 115
Museum of Modern Art 108
Museum of Television & Radio 108
Museum of the City of New York 114
Neighborhoods 87
New York Aquarium (Aquarium for
Wildlife Conservation) 116
New York Botanical Garden 117
New York Convention
and Visitors Bureau 87
New York Hall of Science 120
New York Stock Exchange 97
Radio City Music Hall 104
Rockefeller Center .103
Roosevelt Island Aerial Tramway 105
F.A.O. Schwarz 104
South Street Seaport 97
Staten Island Ferry .98

Statue of Liberty 94
Sylvia's Restaurant 115
United Nations Headquarters 101
World Trade Center 93

BRONX

Long Island Sound

QUEENS

LONG ISLAND

KLYN

OCEAN

Ms. Rooney says:

Find out what's going on in the city first. Phone or stop in at the *New York Convention and Visitors Bureau*. They'll tell you about events, hotels that give discounts to children, and child-friendly restaurants . . . and give you maps. It's the place to plan your trip.

---

2 Columbus Circle, (212) 397-8200

Mr. Bell, the gym teacher, says:

Get on your sneakers and WALK! A few of my favorite places are these:

• *Chinatown*—Stop in for a fortune cookie or, better still, stay for dim sum at one of the restaurants. Play ticktacktoe with a live

chicken at 8 Mott Street. Eat some litchi ice cream.

- *Little Italy*—Try a cannoli at Ferrara's bakery on Grand Street . . . or spaghetti in one of the restaurants.
- *Lower Manhattan*—See the financial center.
- *Greenwich Village*—Take a look at Washington Square Park.
- *Midtown*—Walk along Fifth Avenue. Look up at the Empire State Building. Buy a hot dog from a street vendor.
- *Tribeca and SoHo*—Check out the art galleries.
- *Yorkville*—Eat a German sausage. Try some sauerkraut.

Beast says:

Get me to a baseball game. That means I want to be in New York City anytime between April and October.

The *New York Mets*
Shea Stadium at 126th Street and Roosevelt Avenue, Flushing, Queens. For ticket information, call (718) 507-8499.

The *New York Yankees*
Yankee Stadium at 161st Street and River Avenue in the Bronx. For ticket information, call (718) 293-6000.

And Noah Greene says:

If you're really into baseball, stop in at the *New York Mets Clubhouse Shop* or the *New York Yankees Clubhouse*. They have baseball cards and sweatshirts, and you can see stuff that belonged to your favorite old-time players. You can get your tickets for games here too.

Mets: 575 Fifth Avenue at Forty-seventh Street, (212) 986-4887
Yankees: 110 East Fifty-ninth Street between Park and Lexington Avenues, (212) 758-7844

Mr. Mancina says:

On a sunny day, take a *Circle Line Cruise*. It's a great three-hour boat ride around Manhattan. Munch on a hot dog. The guide will point out the sights.

Pier 83, West Forty-second Street at the Hudson River, (212) 563-3200

Sherri Dent says:

After the cruise, check out the *Intrepid Sea-Air-Space Museum* a few blocks north. The USS *Intrepid* was a World War II aircraft carrier. It's huge! It has space vehicles and rockets, and smaller planes on the deck. You'll see the fastest spy plane in the world. Then take a look at the USS *Edson*, a destroyer. Wait in line to board the USS *Growler*, a guided missile submarine. Find out what it's like inside.

Pier 86, West Forty-sixth Street at Twelfth Avenue, (212) 245-0072

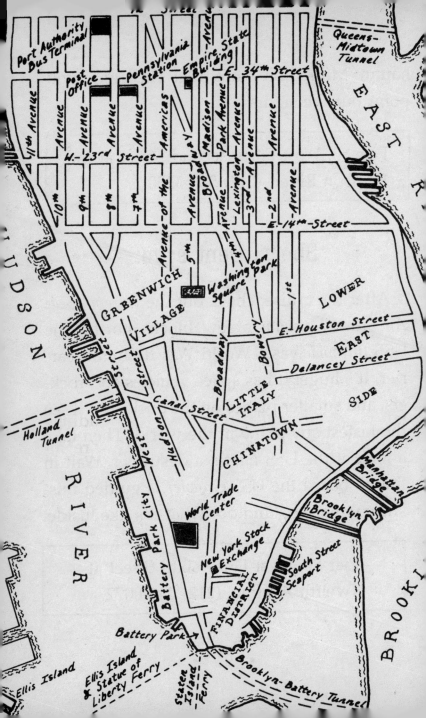

Derrick Grace says:

Whoosh up to the top of the *World Trade Center* in an elevator. Listen to the wind howl as you take the one-minute ride. You can see almost sixty miles on a clear day, and a skillion lights at night.

> Church and Cortlandt Streets,
> (212) 323-2340

Jason Bazyk says:

Check out *Battery Park City* across from the World Trade Center, and the four buildings of the World Financial Center. They're all connected. There are shops to visit and places to eat. The Winter Garden Atrium with its palm trees will make you think you're in Hawaii.

> Battery Park City at Liberty and Vesey Streets, (212) 945-0505

Alex Walker says:

Take a ferry to the *Statue of Liberty* in New York Harbor. It was a gift from the people of France. The American people spent $250,000

for the pedestal . . . and some of it was from pennies donated by schoolchildren. The Statue of Liberty is a goddess who holds a torch. She was the first thing many of the immigrants saw when they reached America . . . and they knew they had reached the land of freedom. You can see the views from her crown.

Liberty Island, (212) 363-3200

Mrs. Barbiero says:

It's wonderful to see the *Ellis Island Immigration Museum.* Many of you had great-grandparents who came from other countries. They stopped here for health checkups before they were allowed to come into the country. You can see pictures of immigrants wearing old-fashioned clothes. Who knows?

Maybe there's a picture of someone from your family.

Ellis Island, (212) 363-7620

Linda Lorca writes:

See *Federal Hall National Memorial and Museum.* Look at the statue of George Washington, our first president. In 1789 he took the oath of office on this spot. Did you know that New York City was the capital of our country then? Inside you can see historical exhibits and buy a souvenir.

26 Wall Street, (212) 264-8711

Wayne O'Brien says:

And right in the same area is the *New York Stock Exchange.* Watch the brokers at work. Hold your ears. It's noisy.

Visitors Center, 20 Broad Street,
(212) 656-5165

Jill Simon says:

I absolutely love the *South Street Seaport.* Sometimes there's entertainment right in the street. You'll see the piers and historic ships. Best of all are the things to eat.

19 Fulton Street at the East River, (212) 732-7678

Jill wants to remind you:

Take a trip to *Staten Island* on the *Staten Island Ferry*. See the tugboats and barges in the harbor, the Statue of Liberty, and the Manhattan skyline.

Battery Park and Whitehall Street, (212) 806-6940

And Mrs. Simon says:

Stop in at the *Lower East Side Tenement Museum*. Poor people lived here when they first came to this country. You can see photographs and exhibits. There are even two apartments set up so you can see how they lived.

> 90 Orchard Street, (212) 431-0233

Noni, Dawn's grandmother, says:

Maybe you'd like to see the *Forbes Magazine Galleries*. See the toy soldiers, and the boats . . . and some other unusual exhibits.

> 62 Fifth Avenue at Twelfth Street, (212) 206-5548

Mrs. Clark loves:

The *Empire State Building*. It has 6,500 windows and 1,860 steps. Take the elevator to the 86th floor for an outside view, or to the 102nd floor for the indoor observatory. You'll see five states on a clear day . . . and five jillion tourists.

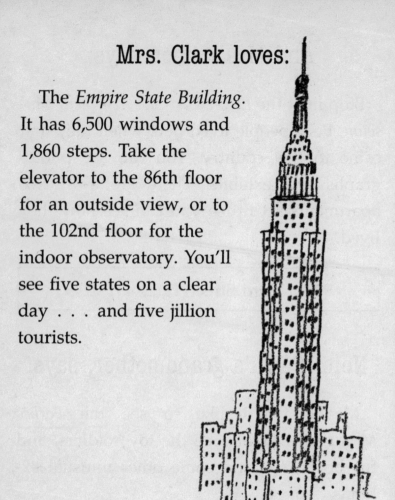

Thirty-fourth Street and Fifth Avenue, (212) 736-3100

Beast says:

All aboard at *Grand Central Terminal*. And even if you don't catch a train, look up at the stars on the lobby ceiling. Matthew and I tested the "whispering wall." It's on the lower level near the Oyster Bar. I faced the wall at one of the four tile arches. Matthew stood facing the wall where the other end of the arch meets the floor. I whispered, "Ruffaroo." Guess what? He heard me. "Ruffaroo to you," he said.

Lexington Avenue and East Forty-second Street, (212) 935-3960

Timothy Barbiero says:

You have to see the *United Nations Headquarters*. Here people from many countries meet to solve the world's problems. Sometimes you can watch them in action if the

General Assembly is in session. Visit the souvenir shop for gifts from all over the world.

East Forty-fifth and East Forty-sixth Streets at the East River, (212) 963-7713

Dawn Bosco says:

Of course you have to visit *Rockefeller Center*. At Christmas, the lights on the tree sparkle like my new earrings. There are neat places to see, the props and makeup room at the NBC Studios and the ice-skaters at the rink. Best of all are the Rockettes at

Radio City Music Hall. I can kick almost as high as they can.

East Forty-seventh to East Fifty-second Street between Fifth Avenue and Avenue of the Americas (Sixth Avenue),
(212) 632-4000

Dawn Bosco says also:

Take me straight to *F.A.O. Schwarz.* It's incredible. Check out the Lego section, the dolls, the toys, the books. Don't be afraid to touch. They love kids. (I'm not crazy about the long lines at Christmastime.)

767 Fifth Avenue at Fifty-eighth Street,
(212) 644-9400

Alex says:

Like to be up high? Take the *Roosevelt Island Aerial Tramway*. It's a car that whooshes from Manhattan to Roosevelt Island and back, right over the East River. You'll see the skyscrapers the way the birds do.

Second Avenue between East Fifty-ninth and East Sixtieth Streets, (212) 832-4543

Mrs. Miller, "The Killer," the substitute teacher, says:

Get yourself over to *Central Park*. Stop at the visitors' center first for maps and to find out what's doing. Then head for the statue of Alice in Wonderland, and see the Cheshire Cat, the White Rabbit, and the Mad Hatter. Check out the Delacorte Clock. A six-animal band plays a tune every half hour. Don't forget to ride the carousel with its painted

horses . . . it's fast! You can feed the ducks on one pond and watch the sailboats on another. You might want to rent a bike and ride safely on roads that are closed to traffic on some hours during the week and on the weekends. Fly a kite in the Sheep Meadow or row around the lake. During the winter, you can ice-skate at the Wollman Memorial Rink. When the ice season ends, roller-skate in the same place. Stop at the zoo. Say hello to the seals, the penguins, and the rest of the gang!

Central Park runs from Fifty-ninth Street to 110th Street and is bordered by Fifth Avenue and Central Park West.

Central Park Wildlife
• Center—East Sixty-fourth Street and Fifth Avenue, (212) 861-6030
• Delacorte Clock—East Sixty-fifth and Fifth Avenue
• Duck Pond—East Fifty-ninth Street and Fifth Avenue
• Loeb Boathouse—Seventy-fourth Street, (212) 861-4137
• Sailboat Pond (Conservatory Water)—East Seventy-fourth Street and Fifth Avenue
• Sheep Meadow—Sixty-seventh Street
• Visitors' Center, The Dairy—Sixty-fourth Street, (212) 794-6564
• Wollman Rink—Sixty-third Street, (212) 396-1010

More inside Central Park:

• Alice in Wonderland—East Seventy-sixth Street and Fifth Avenue

• Bicycles—Rental at Loeb Boathouse

• Carousel—Sixty-fifth Street Transverse, (212) 879-0244

Beast likes:

The *Museum of Television & Radio*. Watch and listen to your old favorites.

25 West Fifty-second Street between Fifth Avenue and Avenue of the Americas (Sixth Avenue), (212) 621-6800

Emily likes:

The *Museum of Modern Art*. You will see artwork that is different and surprising: paintings, photography, drawings, prints,

and a garden full of statues. You might see a film about some of the artwork. Maybe you'll even buy an art print in the gift shop.

11 West Fifty-third Street between Fifth Avenue and Avenue of the Americas (Sixth Avenue), (212) 708-9480

Miss Kara, the art teacher, says:

I really like the *American Craft Museum*. You'll see quilts, and baskets, and things made of clay and glass.

40 West Fifty-third Street between Fifth Avenue and Avenue of the Americas (Sixth Avenue), (212) 956-3535

Alex wants to tell you:

Don't miss the *American Museum of Natural History*. I don't know which I like best, the dinosaurs (one of them is five stories tall), the Naturemax Theater with a giant screen, the animal dioramas (elephants, lions, and tigers), or the Hall of Ocean Life (a model of a blue whale hangs from the ceiling). They have fun classes, programs, and a Kwanzaa festival. At Christmas, there's a tree

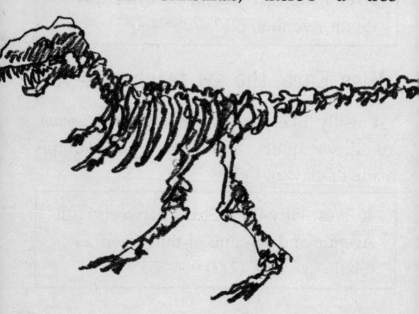

covered with birds and animals made of folded paper. A volunteer will teach you how to make your own.

Central Park West between West Seventy-seventh and West Eighty-first Streets, (212) 769-5100

Ms. Rooney says:

Did I tell you about *Lincoln Center for the Performing Arts*? It's a celebration of performing arts in eight separate buildings. You can see behind the scenes at the Metropolitan Opera, listen to an outdoor concert, watch ballet and other kinds of dance, and hear the world's best music.

140 West Sixty-fifth Street, (212) 546-2656

Miss Kara says:

Wait until you see the *Solomon R. Guggenheim Museum*. It has a spiral shape . . . almost like the inside of a snail. Go to the top in an elevator. Walk down on the ramp to see the paintings, photographs, sculpture, and other artwork.

> East Eighty-eighth Street and Fifth
> Avenue, (212) 423-3500

Emily Arrow says:

The *Metropolitan Museum of Art* is one of the greatest museums in the world. Beautiful paintings are there, as well as statues, mummies, and a real Egyptian temple. Don't miss the arms and armor. At Christmas there's a tree decorated with wonderful ornaments.

1000 Fifth Avenue between East Eighty-second and Eighty-fourth Streets,
(212) 879-5500

Jill says:

I think the *Children's Museum of Manhattan* is terrific. Make your own TV shows. See what's going on in the theater. Learn about recycling and use worms (yuck) to make better soil. Stop in at the gift shop for souvenirs.

212 West Eighty-third Street,
(212) 721-1234

Miss Stewart,
the student teacher, says:

Another great museum is the *Museum of the City of New York*. It has wonderful doll-houses and old toys. You can find out what New York was like a couple of hundred years ago.

103rd Street and Fifth Avenue,
(212) 534-1672

Noah says:

I like *El Museo del Barrio*. It means "the museum of the neighborhood." It has paintings and interesting art and carvings that have to do with Latin American people and their culture.

1230 Fifth Avenue, (212) 831-7272

Alex says:

I love the *Harlem Spirituals, Inc., Tour*. You can go to church to hear cool singing . . . then have a soul food breakfast at *Sylvia's*. Other good tours are *Harlem Your Way!* and *Harlem Renaissance Tours*.

Harlem Renaissance Tours,
(212) 722-9534
Harlem Spirituals, (212) 302-2594
Sylvia's Restaurant, (212) 996-0660
Harlem Your Way, (212) 690-1687

Emily says:

I love the *Cloisters* on the Hudson River. Take a bus or a subway to the Bronx. This building is rebuilt from very old monasteries brought to the United States from Europe. You'll see statues and plants outside, and tapestries inside. They're all about a unicorn.

Fort Tryon Park, (212) 923-3700

Dawn says:

The *New York Aquarium*, now called the *Aquarium for Wildlife Conservation*, in Coney Island is the place for me. It's not Florida, but it has penguins and seals, the beach and the boardwalk.

Surf Avenue at West Eighth Street, Coney Island, Brooklyn, (718) 265-3474

And Emily says:

I wouldn't want you to miss the *New York Botanical Garden*. It has a glass house, and flowers and trees. It has a wonderful growing smell. Best of all, you can find out about plants, and buy some too.

Bronx Park, 200th Street and Southern Boulevard, Bronx, (718) 220-8700

Noni, Dawn's grandmother, says:

How about the *Brooklyn Children's Museum*? It's the first museum for children ever.

There are a playroom and a music room. You'll see science, nature, and environmental exhibits. There are lots of things to touch.

> 145 Brooklyn Avenue, Brooklyn,
> (718) 735-4431

Miss Kara says:

See the *Jewish Museum*. It is in a beautiful château with paintings and objects related to Jewish history.

> 1109 Fifth Avenue at East Ninety-second Street, (212) 423-3200

Ms. Rooney says:

Make sure you save energy for the *Bronx Zoo*, now called the *International Wildlife Conservation Park*. This is the oldest and largest zoo in the country. You can visit the sea lions,

and go into an indoor rain forest to see the monkeys. Take a monorail to see the elephants, rhinoceros, and Siberian tigers. Don't miss the snake in the reptile house. Go over to the Children's Zoo too. Don't think you can see everything in a day. Four thousand animals live here.

Bronx Park, south of East Fordham Road, Bronx, (718) 367-1010

Mr. O'Brien, Wayne's grandfather, says:

Wait a minute. Don't forget about something to see in Queens. How about the *New York Hall of Science*? You can touch, feel, move, and bounce the objects. You might even find out what an atom looks like.

47-10 111th Street, Corona, Queens, (718) 699-0675

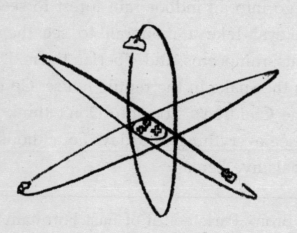